Grandpa's Treasure Box

This book is dedicated to my nieces, Jaclyn and Kimberly.

Pauline Tsui

Cover design by Pauline Tsui
Book design by Stanley Ki
Printed in China

Library of Congress Cataloging in Publication Data

Tsui, Pauline
The Adventures of the Precious Pollabies: Grandfather's Treasure Box / by Pauline Tsui Summary: The story of Asian-American twin sisters who embark on a magical journey with the help of an extraordinary box given to them by their grandfather.
ISBN 978-1-60461-723-8
[1. Fantasy – Fiction. 2. Adventure – Fiction. 3. Children's book]

Acknowledgements

I wish to express my deep appreciation to Patricia Murphy who is my first reader to give her support and encouragement; to Cinda Ely who provided editorial advice; no less to Terese Bartholomew, John Stucky, Nancy Coopersmith, Coral, Paula, Allison, Hakim, Zita, Donna, Michelle, and those of you whose names I have not mentioned, for all your inspiration and invaluable contributions, without which I could not have created this book and the *Precious Pollabies*® dolls.

I thank my parents the most of all, for having taught-by-example, for raising me to be creative, confident, compassionate, and encouraging me to be free to pursue my dreams.

THE ADVENTURE OF BOBO + TASHI

Grandpa's Treasure Box

An original *Precious Pollabies*® tale by Pauline Tsui

Chapter 1

Bobo and Tashi are twin sisters. They live with Mommy and Daddy in San Francisco.

One day they come home from school to find Grandma and Grandpa waiting for them. Each year the grandparents travel around, and always finish their journey by paying the twins a visit. Bobo and Tashi love it when, at the end of the evening, Grandpa tells them wonderful stories about their travels in far-away lands.

As always, Grandpa brings them a special present.

"I found this in a small antique shop in China. It is a Treasure Box, and I hope you girls will put it to good use and fill it with nice things."

Bobo and Tashi love the Treasure Box that Grandpa brought them.

"Bobo, what do you think we should put inside this box?" asks Tashi. "Mommy says we could put our favorite things in it, but it is too small for your books or your favorite toy!"

Bobo loves to read and to play chess. She also loves stuffed animals and her favorite one is a teddy bear named Aiden, which was a present from Daddy when she was two years old.

"What do you have to put in it, Tashi?" says Bobo. "Maybe you can put a small drawing inside, but certainly it won't hold your ballet shoes or your dance costume!"

Tashi loves to draw and to dance. And her favorite play pal is Mommy's pet bunny rabbit named Roe. (Roe is pronounced like row-ee, as in Chloe)

Chapter 2

That night while the twins are in bed, Bobo hears a gentle tapping sound. It seems to be coming from inside the Treasure Box.

Tashi hears it too. She is curious, "Bobo, do you hear what I hear?"

Following the sound Bobo cautiously reaches out to unlock the tiny doors of the box. While the two girls look inside, they see that the opening of the box has become larger.

At the same time, they hear a voice from inside that says, "You may enter."

Not knowing how to respond and wondering where the voice is coming from, Bobo and Tashi take each other's hands and find themselves running down a pathway into the box. They have not had time to think whether the box has become larger or they have grown smaller. They are drawn toward the voice which has a commanding tone, and yet it also sounds very warm and reassuring.

Chapter 3

Once they get out of the far side of the box, Bobo and Tashi find someone waiting for them – a dragon with a big grin on his face, gesturing for them to come closer.

At any other time and place one might wonder how it is that one could come face to face with a dragon and actually talk to him. With Bobo and Tashi, they feel natural even when they meet this dragon for the first time. There is an air of serenity and friendliness about his eyes. Something about the cool breeze and the refreshing scent in the surrounding atmosphere makes them feel quite at home.

"I am the Dragon Gatekeeper and Protector of this land. You have been summoned here to help the people in our village. An evil lord has taken over; he destroys all the trees and the parks and forces the villagers to work for him in building his fortress.

He also orders that the children must be sent away to work in a hard-labor camp once they reach the age of ten."

"The villagers Ah-Wah and Ah-Ying have a son Tong-tong who has a special condition with his hands. Tong-tong used to play wonderful music, but since he suffers from malnutrition his fingers get knotted up each time he tries to use them."

"Ah-Wah has been taken away by the Evil Lord while Ah-Ying has to work in the fields. They have been trying to hide Tong-tong so he doesn't get sent to camp."

"Tong-tong will be turning ten years old in fourteen days and the Evil Lord has already sent word that his soldiers will be coming to take him. I know of a cure that can help Tong-tong but we need your help to get it. The two of you will go to the Sacred Mountains of the West to find this cure. There will be guiding signs that can help you find the way."

"You must reach the mountains and bring back the cure to our village by Tong-tong's birthday, otherwise there will be serious consequences."

"But Mommy never lets us go out on our own!" "How do we know what signs to look for?" the twins say simultaneously.

"Calm down, girls!" says Dragon. "I will summon help for you. Bobo, Tashi, close your eyes and think of a friend dearest to you."

Dragon casts his spell and, a few moments later, says, "Now open your eyes."

Bobo and Tashi open their eyes and look where Dragon is pointing. Out in the distance they can still see the doors of the Treasure Box. Then suddenly the doors pop open, and two bodies come running toward them.

The twins give out a cry of excitement. Bobo and Tashi cannot be happier; their favorite companions Bunny Roe and Teddy Aiden have answered their call and come to help them. Dragon then explains to them about the magical power of the Treasure Box which will be useful for this unusual mission.

"The Treasure Box can take you to different places through different times. Before we go to the Sacred Mountains we must first look for some guiding signs. I will show you where you need to go. Follow me!"

Chapter 4

Bobo, Tashi, Roe and Aiden follow Dragon back into the Treasure Box.

Once inside, Dragon's two bulging green eyes light up like two glowing emeralds. As they get used to the dimness of the enclosed box, they begin to see what look like ancient writings on the wall. There also appears to be a map and some mysterious colored markings.

Dragon points to a blue marking on the map with his claw-like finger. He utters some magical words which sound like something between a growl and a gentle roar that only a dragon could utter.

The ride within the box is smooth and short. With a firm nod Dragon indicates to the four young travelers that they have arrived at the first stop-point of their journey. Bobo, Tashi and their two friends step out of the box to find themselves in front of a large lake. "What are we looking for here?" the twins wonder.

Dragon's voice from inside the box says, "Ask Turtle."

Chapter 5

Aiden is the first to speak out: "The first guiding sign must be in this lake, and Dragon is indicating to us that the clue is through a turtle."

The four travelers see some buildings in the distance. They walk toward the buildings and come to a water village called Suzhou. Amidst the small canals and garden pavilions they find an old turtle. The turtle tells the travelers he will help them if they play three games of chess with him. Bobo accepts his challenge. Turtle and Bobo each win one set of chess, then Bobo wins the third.

To keep his promise Turtle leads the four travelers back to the lake, and calls upon two fish to help Bobo find the guiding sign.

"You've won the game so now you will complete this task by yourself!" Turtle says.

Tashi, Aiden and Roe gather anxiously by the shore as they watch Bobo dive into the lake to follow the fish. The fish lead Bobo to the bottom of the lake where she finds a big white pearl.

Afterwards, Bobo thanks the fish and returns to shore with the Pearl in her hands. Tashi, Aiden and Roe are very pleased to see her resurface from the lake.

Bobo's clothes have gotten all wet so the villagers bring her some dry new clothes. One villager gives Bobo a pair of yellow tiger shoes, telling her that in the Chinese tradition tiger shoes bring protective power and ward off evil spirits.

In her bright red Chinese costume and yellow tiger shoes, Bobo happily leads the group back to the Treasure Box with the big White Pearl wrapped in a silk handkerchief.

Chapter 6

Once inside the Treasure Box, Dragon points his claw to a green marking on the map and utters the magical words. This time the Treasure Box takes the travelers to a bamboo forest.

The bamboo trees are jade green in color. Their branches shoot up to the sky and waver as the wind blows making rustling sounds.

As the four walk into the bamboo grove Roe, who has sharp hearing due to her long pointy ears, hears a faint sound of someone struggling.

They follow the sound and find a horse caught in between the tangled bamboo branches crying for help.

Bobo and Tashi pull very hard to separate the bamboo branches while Roe and Aiden free the horse from her entanglement.

The horse, whose name is Marnie, is so happy to be rescued that she asks to join the travelers in their quest. They all return to the Treasure Box together, ready for the next part of their journey.

Chapter 7

On the third day of their journey, Dragon points his claw to an amber marking on the map. When the five travelers come out of the box they find themselves in a desert area in front of some stone-like ruins. They have arrived in a lost petrified city.

"Look for fu-dogs." Dragon says.

The five of them search among the stone structures and find statues of humans and animals. Eventually, they come to a statue that looks like a giant fu-dog with a small fu-dog at its side.

There are some writings on the pedestal of the statue. Marnie helps them decipher the writing which gives them the secret to unlock the city of stone.

Following the writing, the five of them wait until the moon rises to the center of the sky. Bobo then takes out her big White Pearl and collects the moonbeam that shines upon it. The Pearl deflects the beam of light and casts a light upon every stone structure and statue in the ruins.

When morning comes, the city of ruins comes back to life.

The giant fu-dog is actually a Tibetan apso and the little fu-dog is its puppy, named Chukm.

The people of the lost city are so grateful to be revived after years of petrification that they give Chukm to the travelers to aid them on their journey. (Chukm is pronounced chum, as in drum)

Chapter 8

Back inside the Treasure Box Dragon points to a purple marking and utters his magical roar. Once again the box takes the travelers to their next destination.

Before they leave the Treasure Box, Dragon gives them a warning, "This part of the land is at a high altitude, which means that the air will be thin and you may get light in the head. Look for signs of danger and stay focused on your mission. First go find some food to fill your stomachs. Your bodies need proper nourishment for good energy."

Bobo and Tashi walk hand-in-hand followed by Roe, Aiden, Marnie and Chukm. At the side of the road they find a small teahouse that serves tea, noodles and sweet cakes.

After a nice, hearty meal the six of them follow the road that leads across a plateau into a hilly area. As they walk past the first hill they come to an open area where they are dazzled by a beautiful scene.

Hundreds and thousands of purple butterflies fly above their heads.
Some land on their shoulders and their hands, hoofs and paws.
The butterflies seem to be growing out of a large willow tree;
their tiny bodies with fluttering wings stem out of the tree branches.
As they flutter their wings the tree branches move with them.

Bobo, Tashi and their friends all watch with amazement.

After a while Bobo says, "We should get going."

"No, let's stay." says Tashi. "Perhaps the tree of purple butterflies is a sign of some sort. Besides, I want to watch some more, it is such a pretty sight!"

It is the first time that Tashi has disagreed with her sister since the beginning of their journey. Even though the twins have differences in their personalities, they have always managed to find a middle ground.

"Yes, let's stay a few minutes longer." Roe and Aiden exclaim together. "We have walked for so long our feet are getting tired."

Bobo cannot argue against the rest of them who all want to stay. They sit down on the grass and, one by one, become light-headed, their eyelids getting heavy.

Soon they lie down and fall into a deep sleep.

Chapter 9

Finally the sound of Dragon's voice wakes them from their sleep.

The purple butterflies have disappeared out of sight. The butterflies have all detached themselves and flown away leaving behind the willow tree with its bare branches.

"I have called you many times. The purple butterflies must have carried my voice into the hills and away from you. You have been sleeping for seven days! Get up, there is little time left!"

Bobo and Tashi feel very bad about losing their focus, and for the first time fear they might fail in their mission.

Roe says, "We have all made a big mistake. The important thing is to look ahead. We cannot lose any more time. Let's get moving!"

So they all pull themselves together and Bobo, Tashi, Roe, Aiden, Marnie and Chukm get ready to set off on their journey again.

As they are about to leave, Chukm sniffs and finds something beneath the willow tree. After digging into the soil they discover a purple amulet in the shape of a butterfly.

Tashi takes it and puts it inside her pocket.

Chukm is an excellent pathfinder because of his sharp sense of smell and awareness of the surroundings. He soon leads them out of the hilly area and back to the Treasure Box where Dragon anxiously awaits them.

Chapter 10

Everyone goes inside the Treasure Box again, and Dragon points to a rainbow colored marking on the wall.

"We are now getting very close to the Sacred Mountains of the West, but with every step there is potential danger. There are only four days left. Look for the peacock lady and ask for her help in finding the entrance to the big rock cave."

The travelers find themselves in a green plateau surrounded by mountain ranges; some have snow on the peaks. Across the plateau they find some nomads in front of a beautiful white tent.

A group of children are playing in the open field while the men and women are busy preparing for some kind of celebration.

"Please, can you tell us where to find the peacock lady?" Bobo asks around but no one seems to know the answer.

"We don't know of any peacock lady. There is a monastery at the foot of the mountains, perhaps someone there will know. Why don't you join us for our Spring Festival and we will take you there in the morning."

That evening, Bobo, Tashi and their companions accept the nomads' hospitality and join their spring celebration.

The ladies invite Tashi to join them in their dance. They dress her up in a lovely Tibetan robe with a color-striped apron.

Bobo and the animals sit in a big circle and chant to the dancers.

Chapter 11

The next morning the nomads fold up their tent and take the travelers to the foot of the Sacred Mountains. Bobo and Tashi thank their hosts and say goodbye to their new nomad friends. When they approach the monastery they find the doors have been locked from the outside and the place seems deserted.

They walk around to the side, and there under some bushes see an elderly woman with peacocks around her.

"Good morning. Could you tell us where the entrance to the big rock cave is?" Bobo and Tashi address the woman with the peacocks.

Without even looking up at the travelers, the elderly woman answers in a coarse voice, "Why should I tell you? You haven't done anything for me!"

Bobo and Tashi give each other a glance, remembering that Mommy says always be polite, even to strangers.

"What would you like us to do for you?" The twins say together.

The peacock lady has them sweep the floor, feed the peacocks and weed the grass. By noon the twins have completed all the chores. What more can she possibly ask them to do? Aiden and Roe are getting worried about the passing of time.

"This will be your last chore. I want to have my peacocks stretch out their tails. All you need to do is make them spread their tail feathers."

Now it has been said that peacocks spread their tail feathers only when they see something beautiful and wonderful in front of them. But no matter what the twins and their animal friends do, they cannot make the peacocks spread their tails.

Tashi has an idea. She pulls out the purple butterfly amulet and offers it to the peacock lady.

As she hands it to her, a burst of white dust shoots out of the amulet and falls through the air. A beautiful rainbow appears before them as the crystalline dust catches the sunlight.

The peacocks respond by spreading out their beautiful tail feathers.

The peacock lady is very pleased with the travelers.

"Follow the direction of the rainbow for a hundred yards and you will see a big rock cave. The cure is inside this cave. Bring it back to me and I shall tell you how to prepare it. Each one of you must carry a peacock feather to protect yourselves from any poisonous gas or hostile creature," the peacock lady says and she gives each one of them a peacock feather.

After they bid farewell to the peacock lady, the travelers hurry toward the direction of the rainbow.

Bobo, Tashi, and their animal companions soon come to the opening of the rock cave. At the entrance they see rocks of unusual shapes and colors. As they go deeper into the cave, the light becomes dimmer and they soon find themselves in total darkness.

Bobo takes out the big White Pearl which glows in the dark, and with its light they make their way further into the cave.

Marnie finds a flight of steps and they climb up to see where it leads.

Up and up they go. They notice that the huge pillars of stone around them begin to take on a frosted surface and then turn icy.

A while later they become giant icicles. There are large and small caves alongside the ice pillars and they walk through cave after cave to search for the cure.

Finally, Aiden points to a small crack between the pillars and discovers a small cave. Inside there is a Snow Lotus flower encased in a pillar of ice.

They all get very excited, "Yes! We have found the cure. Yes!"

But how will they get the Snow Lotus out of the ice pillar? Their joy and excitement only last a second, and then there is silence.

"Think, Bobo, think what to do." Bobo knocks on her little head with her tiny knuckles.

"Think, Tashi, think. Do we have any more magic charms?" Tashi looks around for anything that could break the ice.

Then they hear Dragon's voice from afar, "Summon the tigers."

"What tigers?" Before Bobo can understand what Dragon is saying, she instinctively looks down and sees her bright yellow tiger shoes.

"Let us help," the tiger shoes speak to Bobo.

In an instant two gigantic beasts spring out of the tip of Bobo's shoes and start gnawing at the ice pillar which holds the Snow Lotus.

The two tigers use their sharp teeth and claws to break away a chunk of ice with the Snow Lotus inside. They are careful to bite only the edges of the ice so as not to damage the flower petals.

The travelers then carry the chunk of ice down the steps and out of the cave to return to the peacock lady's place.

Chapter 13

The peacock lady applauds the travelers for their find. She tells them, "The Snow Lotus is the essence of life medicine that can cure any disease when used with the White Pearl. You have done well to find the cure but now you must melt the ice and defrost the Snow Lotus to bring it back for your patient. You have only one day left so you must act quickly."

Bobo and Tashi gather all the dry wood that they can find while Aiden and Roe build a fire to melt the big chunk of ice. The ice takes a long time to melt.

"Make a bigger fire. We have to melt it to release the cure!"

Everyone tries hard to find more wood to bring up the heat. Soon there is nothing left to burn, yet the chunk of ice has barely melted.

Then Aiden makes a very bold move.

There is not a moment to waste. They must extract the Snow Lotus before the day ends. Tong-tong needs their help or soon he will be taken by the soldiers of the Evil Lord.

Aiden gathers the last piece of wood that he could find – the Treasure Box.
It's a big sacrifice, but there is no better choice. He makes a quick
apology to Dragon, then thrusts the box into the fire.

No sooner has he done that than the weak flames are revived and
a huge fire burns before them. They can hear the crackling sound of
the burning wood and see little sparks in the air. Finally the ice is melting! Everyone cheers.
Everyone except Dragon, as both Bobo and Tashi go over and hug him.

Chapter 14

"How are we going to bring the cure back to Tong-tong? How can we be back in time for his tenth birthday? The soldiers will be coming for him by tomorrow morning!" The twins ask themselves but there is no simple answer, they are now thousands of miles away from the village and have just lost their only means of fast transport.

The peacock lady who has been watching them now comes forward, "Weren't you a bit hasty in burning up your Treasure Box? How are you going to get back now?"

Bobo, Tashi, Roe, Marnie and Chukm all speak at the same time, "We stand by Aiden's decision. He has made the right choice. We just have to find another way to go back."

Dragon looks at them, shaking his head, "I have no other magic box to take you back. You better come up with another plan."

The peacock lady says, "My friends, since all of you are united in this unselfish act to protect Tong-tong and his village, I will give you my own magic charm."

Then she hands Tashi a beautiful jade necklace with a red coral heart. "Put it on Marnie."

* * *

The moment has come. Bobo and Tashi feel a strange air
of wonder around them as everything seems to be transformed.
As soon as the twins put the necklace around Marnie's neck it
turns into green jade armor with little red hearts around the neck.

Out of this armor a spread of wings grows. Around them the peacocks all spread
their tail feathers as the peacock lady turns from an elderly woman into a radiant goddess.

"Go now. Marnie can fly you back to your village. Give this to Tong-tong as a present for his tenth birthday." She hands the twins a sheng - a mouth organ made of bamboo.

Bobo, Tashi, Roe, Aiden and Chukm climb onto Marnie's back and, waving goodbye to Dragon and the Goddess, fly away in the direction of the village.

Chapter 14

Bobo, Tashi and their animal friends arrive at the home of Ah-Wah and Ah-Ying. The soldiers are just arriving to take Tong-tong away.

"Wait! Can you give us just a moment?" Tashi pleads with the soldiers while Bobo runs inside.

Bobo takes out the Snow Lotus and White Pearl from the silk handkerchief wrapping and hands them to Ah-Ying. Ah-Ying crushes the Pearl with a rock scepter and puts the powder in a cup of water together with the Lotus petals. Ah-Ying then raises the cup to Tong-tong's lips, from which he drinks to the last drop.

Tashi comes into the house; the soldiers follow closely behind her.

"We have one more thing to give to Tong-tong. Can you please, please give us another moment?" She takes out the sheng and hands it to Tong-tong.

"Would you play us one song?" says Bobo.

As Tong-tong raises the sheng to his lips and puts his fingers on the keys to play a first note, he yells out in surprise, "Mother, my fingers are not crooked anymore! My strength has come back to me!"

Ah-Ying watches her son with awe and joy as Tong-tong begins to play a tune. It is the most beautiful sound ever to be heard by human ears that fills the room. One by one, the faces of the guards are transformed by the sweet melody.

As Tong-tong plays on, the soldiers put away their weapons and sit down to listen. The neighbors come by to listen, and then the birds come too.

The sweet melody then turns into a powerful song that echoes like the roaring waves. The wind carries forth the music and soon it reaches across the fields to the Evil Lord's fortress. It tears down the walls of the fortress, transforms the weapons into yellow wild flowers and melts the barred gates which have kept the workers prisoners.

The Evil Lord cannot bear the sound of the music. Realizing that he no longer has the soldiers at his command, he runs away into the sunset never to be seen again.

Everyone is overjoyed to be rid of the Evil Lord. Ah-Wah and other villagers leave the Evil Lord's castle to reunite with their families. Tong-tong is particularly grateful to Bobo and Tashi for their help.

As the sun shines upon Tong-tong's rosy cheeks, Tashi notices something about his face. She whispers into Bobo's ear, "Hey, doesn't Tong-tong look like someone we know?"

Behind them Bobo and Tashi feel a gentle touch on their backs. Dragon reappears, though no one knows how he has managed to return to the village.

"Girls, it is time for you to go home!" Sensing the question still on Bobo's and Tashi's faces, Dragon gives the twins a reassuring nod.

* * *

Bobo and Tashi wake up in the morning to find themselves back in their own bedroom. Mommy and Daddy are at their side.

"Mommy, you will never guess where we went!" Bobo says.

Together the twins tell Mommy and Daddy how they have gone inside the Treasure Box and helped to save a boy and his village with the aid of their animal friends. Mommy and Daddy agree that it is a good story.

Later that day, Mommy and Daddy sit down with the twins to look through an old family album which Grandpa has left with them. Bobo's and Tashi's jaws drop open as they point to Grandpa's childhood photo.

"That's Tong-tong! Tong-tong is Grandpa!" Now Bobo and Tashi understand why they had such a familiar feeling toward Tong-tong and his village.

"It is all but a dream, a nice dream!" Mommy and Daddy say with a nod and a smile.

But is it?

- The End -

Glossary

Apso – A type of dog native to Tibet believed to bring luck to its owner. For over two thousand years the Lhasa apso was bred by holy men and nobles as a sacred watchdog for temples and monasteries.

Butterfly – Symbolizes blessings and marital happiness.

China – One of the world's oldest continuing civilizations, that is the inventor of paper, printing, the compass and gun powder. A vast and diverse landscape, China has mountains, rivers, deserts and lush forests.

Dragon – An ancient symbol in Chinese mythology; also one of the four protectors of Tibet. The dragon is a symbol of power and a benevolent being that brings rain. It is associated with prosperity and abundance.

Fu-dog – Powerful mythical animal that guards Chinese Imperial palaces, temples and emperors' tombs as protector.

Peacock – A regal bird associated with contentment and grace. In Tibet, peacocks are believed to consume bad spirits and are associated with cleansing.

San Francisco – The state of California's fourth largest city and home of great diversity and cultural wealth.

Sheng – Mouth organ made of bamboo, found in China and other Asian countries.

Snow Lotus – A rare medicinal plant native to China and Tibet.

Spring Festival – Celebrated in cultures throughout the world, spring festivals honor new beginnings and are often associated with the Lunar New Year.

Suzhou – A city in China renowned for its natural scenery and beautifully designed gardens, stone bridges and pagodas. Because of its many waterways it is nicknamed Venice of the East.

Tiger – One of the twelve zodiac animals and a symbol of protection. The stripes on a tiger's forehead look like the Chinese character for king, which is why boys are given shoes decorated with tigers to wear.

Tibet – The highest region on earth often called Roof of the World. Its spiritual leader, the Dalai Lama, is committed to spreading the values of compassion and forgiveness. The Tibetan region was incorporated into the national boundaries of China in 1959, the validity of which is still disputed by many people.

From the author:

The Precious Pollabies are Bobo, Tashi and their animal friends who uphold important values and protect others from harm. "Po" in the word Pollabies refers to the Chinese character which means treasure or something precious; it also means protection.

There are miracles and wonders around us even though most of the time we do not notice them. Moments of love, time spent with family, sounds of laughter from our friends, small bits of nature and beauty in our surroundings. These are no less wonderful than the adventures of the Precious Pollabies. Treasure the little miracles and wonders in your lives.